Brady Brady
and the Ballpark Bark

Written by Mary Shaw
Illustrated by Chuck Temple

PUBLISHED BY
BRADY BRADY INC.

Published in Canada in 2007 by

Brady Brady Inc.
P.O. Box 367
Waterloo, Ontario
Canada
N2J 4A4

Library and Archives Canada Cataloguing in Publication

Shaw, Mary, 1965-
Brady Brady and the ballpark bark / Mary Shaw and Chuck Temple.

ISBN 978-1-897169-10-0

I. Temple, Chuck, 1962- II. Title.
PS8587.H3473B728 2007   jC813'.6   C2007-903086-6

With the season opener only days away,
Tree is swinging like a gate – and missing every time.
Brady is trying to help but Hatrick keeps getting in the way. If only he'd stop barking!

Printed and bound in Canada

The perfect spring day that Brady had been waiting for had finally arrived. He grabbed his bat and glove and headed to the ballpark to meet his new baseball team.

His dog, Hatrick, was excited too! He carried an old baseball in his mouth as he raced out the door with Brady.

Brady was the first to arrive and the first to get a Mudbugs uniform.
He chose his lucky number 4. As his teammates arrived, Brady
high-fived them and Coach handed out more shirts and caps.
Tree was a bit late. The only uniform left was a size extra small.
It just wouldn't do.

"Here, take mine," Coach told him. "You'll never be able to swing a bat in that." He put the extra small shirt in his sports bag. Everyone was happy – until the practice started.

Coach had them run bases to warm up. Hatrick ran too, but he got in the way and tripped Tes.

They threw balls at the fence to improve their accuracy, but Hatrick collected them all.

No one had a chance to catch a single pop fly or grounder.

Coach was watching. "Brady Brady," he called.
"I'm sorry. The dog better go home.
He's a great fan, but he doesn't know much
about baseball."

Brady led Hatrick home, shut him in the house, and hurried back to the
park in time for batting practice.

Tes hit the ball into right field. Kev whacked his into left field.

Brady was up next. He tied his laces in a double knot and headed toward home plate.

He hit the dust off his cleats and took a practice swing. Coach tossed the ball, and Brady swung the bat with all his might.

CRACK!

The ball sailed over Freddie's head toward center field, landing just in front of the fence.

Everyone cheered as he ran the bases.

Next, Coach pitched the ball to Tree. He swung hard – but *before* the ball even crossed home plate. "That's okay, Tree," Brady called from the dugout. Coach pitched again. Tree swung – but *after* the ball crossed home plate.

"You'll get it next time, Tree!" Brady called out again. But Tree missed every pitch that Coach threw.

"Don't worry, it's just a matter of timing," Coach explained to Tree as they walked to the dugout. "Opening day is coming up," he reminded his team. "Everyone has to be ready."

Tree was sure that Coach was talking about him.

"What am I going to do?" Tree said sadly, pulling his ball cap over his face. "I can't hit the ball to save my life!"

"I have a great idea!" Brady said. "We have one week to make you into the best hitter ever."

"WE?" the kids said in unison.

Brady Brady told the kids his plan. "Meet me in my backyard. We have our work cut out for us," he said, winking at Tree.

At home, Brady ran to the backyard shed. He gathered a garden glove, two pylons, a burlap sack, and made a baseball diamond.

Poor Hatrick barked to be let out, but Brady left him in the house so he couldn't bother anyone.

The kids showed up and took their places in the field. As it turned out, they weren't really needed. Tree stood over the burlap sack swinging at every pitch Brady threw – before or after the ball crossed the plate! Brady pitched until he thought his arm would drop off.
Tree didn't hit a single ball.

When it got dark, Brady grabbed some flashlights from the shed,
and the kids took turns holding them.
That way they could work with Tree a little longer.

"Brady Brady, time to wrap it up,"
Brady's mom called from the window.

"It's late, and Hatrick wants out. His barking is driving us **crrraaazy!**"

Tree slumped to the ground. "It's no use," he said sadly. "We could do this all summer, and I still wouldn't connect with the ball!"

Brady lay in bed that night trying to figure out a way to help his friend. Hatrick lay beside him with a baseball in his mouth.

"I know buddy," Brady whispered, "I wish you could help too...."

Brady set up the backyard again the next day. Tree arrived, dragging his bat behind him.

"Maybe the bat's too short," Tes suggested.

"Maybe he's holding it too tight," said Chester.

"Maybe his shoes are on the wrong feet," added Kev.

Hatrick barked wildly from inside the house, but no one paid any attention.

Tree took his place over the burlap sack.

He didn't have any luck on this day, or for the rest of the week. He was starting to panic.

After the kids left, Brady and Tree were trying a few last pitches when the back door opened. "Brady Brady," his dad shouted. "Hatrick needs company. He's been inside, barking all day."

Hatrick ran up to Brady with the baseball in his mouth.

"Not now boy," Brady told him. "Tree has to practice some more."

Hatrick stood against the fence, watching.

Tree shouldered the bat, and Brady threw him a straight pitch. Hatrick waited until the right second and gave a sharp bark. Startled, Tree swung. ***Thwack!***

The ball sailed over the fence. Tree rubbed his eyes to make sure he hadn't imagined the incredible hit.

"Way to go Tree!!" Brady said, "Do it again!"

Tree got set for the next pitch. As the ball crossed the plate, Hatrick barked loudly. Tree swung, and again, the ball sailed out of the yard.

"What's gotten into you?" Brady asked.

"I guess I owe it to you and all this practice," Tree said, beaming. "Oh, and Hatrick, cheering me on."

"That's it!" Brady cried. "It *is* Hatrick! He's telling you when to swing!"

Brady put Hatrick in the house, then pitched to his friend, just like before. Tree went back to his old ways – swing and a miss, swing and a miss.

Brady called Hatrick back outside. Right on cue, Hatrick barked, and Tree crushed the ball over the fence. Tree and Hatrick sent ball after ball out of the yard. The timing was perfect. The season opener was tomorrow!

Opening day was filled with the excited chatter of fans
and the smell of hot dogs.

Tree sat nervously in the dugout making circles in the dust
with his cleats until it was his turn to bat.

"You can do it," Brady said, patting Tree on the back. "With a little help
from your friend." He pointed at the fence behind home plate.

There sat Hatrick, wagging his tail.

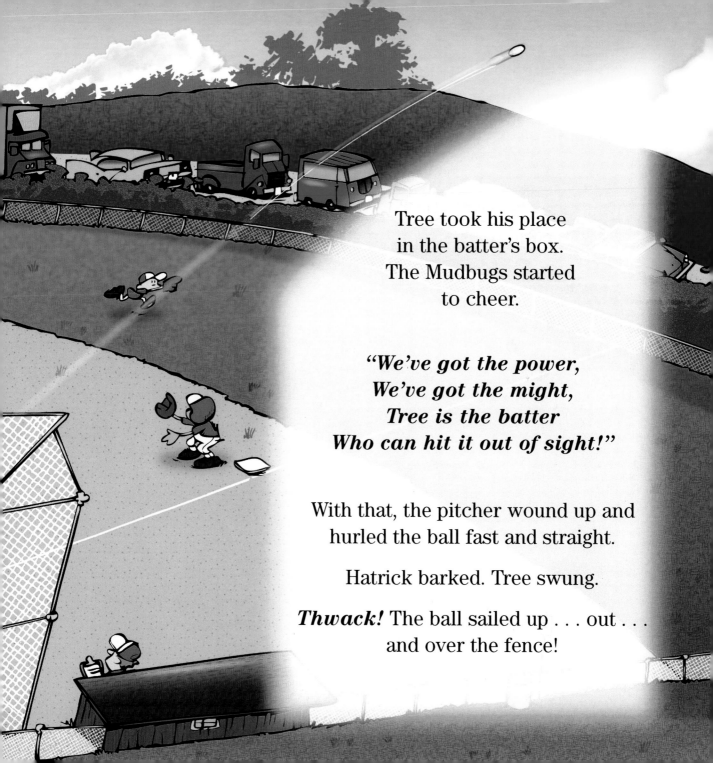

Tree took his place
in the batter's box.
The Mudbugs started
to cheer.

*"We've got the power,
We've got the might,
Tree is the batter
Who can hit it out of sight!"*

With that, the pitcher wound up and
hurled the ball fast and straight.

Hatrick barked. Tree swung.

Thwack! The ball sailed up . . . out . . .
and over the fence!

"Great game, Mudbugs!" Coach said, as they all slurped on treats in the dugout. "I think we're going to have an interesting season."

He reached into his sports bag for the leftover extra small uniform, and put it on Hatrick.

Hatrick, the new Mudbugs' mascot, couldn't have agreed more.